# Kartikeya and Paravani the Peacock

Shubha Vilas

Om KIDZ
An imprint of Om Books International

Tarakasura was a fearsome demon. Brahma had granted him a boon that he could be killed only by someone as powerful as Shiva's son. The unusual boon had made Tarakasura invincible.

He wanted to conquer the fourteen planetary systems of the Universe. To fulfil his ambition, he began to torture the devatas. He created so much misery among them that something definitely had to be done very soon.

Brahma somehow planned Shiva's marriage to Parvati. Soon, Kartikeya was born. This wonder baby had six faces, each representing Shiva's six energies. These energies then united to form a single-faced Kartikeya. Mother Parvati gave him her Shakti in the form of a divine spear called Vela which made him very powerful.

Kartikeya was not only an expert warrior, but full of wisdom too. Once he explained the meaning of OM to his father. Shiva was truly amazed. Parvati was so happy she gave him a new name–Swaminatha–guru of her husband.

Now it was time for Kartikeya to take on the demon Tarakasura and rescue the gods. How could he not win when he had so many gifts? He had a huge army given by Shiva, a magical garland given by Vishnu, a pot full of nectar given by Ganga and a sacred stick gifted by Brihaspati.

The army had 30,000 soldiers, all as powerful as Shiva. The garland gave additional strength to the one who wore it. With so much to protect him, Kartikeya was high on confidence. Nothing could stop him now.

At the entrance of Tarakasura's kingdom, Kartikeya was met by Tarakasura's brother Surpadman and his army. He was no match for Kartikeya.

Surpadman, a powerful demon himself, was surprised that Kartikeya could defeat him so easily. He was now scared for his brother's life. Surely, his brother's life was in danger. He ran to give Tarakasura the alarming news.

Realising that no one could defeat Kartikeya, Tarakasura jumped in to fight the battle. But because Kartikeya was born to kill Tarakasura, he had no trouble in killing him. How much ever he tried, Tarakasura's weapons were useless against Kartikeya.

Kartikeya destroyed every weapon and every trick that Tarakasura used on him. Soon, the demon lay on the floor and the gods celebrated by showering flowers on Kartikeya.

After Tarakasura's death, the entire army caved in. Surpadman had two options. Fight and die, or surrender and live. Fearful for his life, Surpadman surrendered to Kartikeya. Kartikeya felt sorry for him because Surpadman, in his last life, was a devotee of Lord Shiva. His mistakes had given him the life of a demon. Although he should kill him, something was stopping Kartikeya. Perhaps, he did not want to kill his father's devotee. For Surpadman, this was a chance to repent for the mistakes he had done.

He changed his form to become a tree so that he could stand still and perform austerities and ask for forgiveness. Kartikeya, however, thought to complete his task of killing all demons as expected from him. Even if it was a tree. He shot his arrow at the tree, splitting the tree into two halves.

The tree decided to do something unusual. One half of the tree became a rooster and the other half turned into beautiful peacock called Paravani. Kartikeya put the rooster on his flag as an emblem and mounted the peacock. Paravani the Peacock was very happy. His life had completely changed. Kartikeya had chosen him as his vehicle. He himself couldn't believe that once upon a time he had been a dreadful demon!